FAR OUT
CLASSIC STORIES

D0965009

STONE ARCH BOOKS
a capstone imprint

INTRODUCING...

ALICE

QUEENIE HEARTS

MR. WHITE

MADDIE

KITTY

DEE AND DOM

in...

Far Out Classic Stories is published by
Stone Arch Books,
an imprint of Capstone.
1710 Roe Crest Drive
North Mankato, Minnesota 56003
www.capstonepub.com

Library of Congress Cataloging-in-
Publication Data is available on the
Library of Congress website.
ISBN: 978-1-4965-8684-1 (hardcover)
ISBN: 978-1-4965-9192-0 (paperback)
ISBN: 978-1-4965-8685-8 (eBook PDF)

Summary: Alice is a super-serious
pre-teen secret agent, but her new
team at Wonderland is . . . odd.
Mr. White, the new boss, is always
running late. Maddie makes wacky spy
hats. And Alice's new partner, Kitty,
keeps disappearing. How can Alice stop
the evil Queenie Hearts's top-secret
plan amid all this madness?

Designed by Hilary Wacholz
Edited by Abby Huff
Lettered by Jaymes Reed

Printed and bound in the USA.
PA99

FAR OUT CLASSIC STORIES

ALICE, SECRET AGENT OF WONDERLAND

A GRAPHIC NOVEL

BY KATIE SCHENKEL

ILLUSTRATED BY FERN CANO

Maddie, our mad scientist and inventor of gadgets.

Code name: The Hatter

Very nice to meet you, Alice!

And last but not least, your new partner—

Oh!

It seems Kitty has disappeared again.

"Again"?

No matter. You'll meet her in due time.

Right now, you're late for your training session with the twins!

Why are you smiling like that?

Wait, you're Alice! It all makes sense now.

No reason. You're just a funny sort of girl.

Excuse me, I am *not* funny.

I'm here to be a professional spy. I take my work seriously, unlike everyone else in this—

Alice, there you are.

Oh good, I see you finally met Kitty!

Because I want to be the best spy in the world. Mr. White's letter made Wonderland sound like the perfect place to do that.

But it'll never happen if my teammates are completely *mad.*

I can't help with that. Everyone is a little mad in Wonderland. Even *you.*

I am *NOT* mad.

You must be, or you wouldn't still be here.

HUFF!

Being odd isn't such a bad thing, you know.

Maddie's silliness helps her gadgets be extra clever. The twins' unique moves keep the bad guys on their toes.

Better to be silly than super serious all the time.

I just want things done the *right* way.

Well maybe there are lots of ways to do things.

Gasp! What a *darling* outfit!

We turned away for a second, and then they were gone.

Find my tarts, and then...

OFF WITH YOUR HEAD!

SWOOSH!

Great, what am I going to do now?

I have some ideas.

GAH!

Hey, Alice.

Cheshire Cat? You can turn *invisible*?!

Yep. It's all thanks to Maddie's wonderful hat technology.

Sorry I skipped the party. I was grabbing the tarts while you distracted Queenie.

Stop right there!

Congrats, team!

And congrats to Alice, the newest member of our little family.

Totally.

And to celebrate, I've made new hats for everyone!

Are you sure this party isn't too *maddening* for you?

You know what ...

A little madness can be a good thing.

ALL ABOUT THE ORIGINAL STORY!

Alice's Adventures in Wonderland by Lewis Carroll is a novel first published in 1865. The book starts with Alice feeling bored. While reading with her big sister, Alice sees a talking white rabbit saying how he's late to something. Alice follows him down a deep rabbit hole into a strange place called Wonderland.

As Alice looks for the rabbit, she has many odd adventures. First, Alice takes a drink that makes her tiny. Then she eats a cake that makes her giant. She meets a talking caterpillar who is rude and a grinning Cheshire Cat who can disappear. Alice has a tea party with the Mad Hatter and his friends (including a sleepy Dormouse).

Finally, Alice finds the White Rabbit at the Queen of Hearts's garden party. The Queen of Hearts has a bad temper. She shouts, "Off with their heads!" if she doesn't get her way. After someone steals the Queen's tarts, Alice is put on trial and almost loses *her* head! Luckily, that's when Alice wakes up and realizes her time in Wonderland was all a dream.

The book was so successful that Carroll wrote a sequel in 1871 called *Through the Looking-Glass, and What Alice Found There*. Instead of chasing a rabbit, Alice walks through her living room mirror into an opposite world! She meets more strange people, including royal chess pieces, talking flowers, and Tweedledee and Tweedledum. Alice even becomes a queen herself. Once again, the story ends with Alice realizing she'd been asleep the whole time.

The Alice books have been reworked into movies, TV shows, and even video games. Most retellings pull in details from both stories—this comic book does the same thing!

A **FAR OUT** GUIDE TO THE STORY'S SPY TWISTS

Instead of chasing the White Rabbit down the rabbit hole, Alice is invited by Mr. White to join his secret agents.

The disappearing Cheshire Cat is replaced by Kitty, who uses awesome invisibility tech.

The Mad Hatter and Dormouse are switched out for genius inventor Maddie and her baby sister (and intern), Dora.

The Queen of Hearts is bossy royalty. Queenie Hearts is a rich and evil mastermind—and still bossy!

VISUAL QUESTIONS

In your own words, describe what happens between the first panel and the second. Brainstorm other ways you could draw this moment.

Comics aren't always drawn realistically. The artist exaggerated many of the characters' expressions. What do you think of this choice? How does it affect the story's tone? Find at least two other examples of over-the-top expressions in the book.

Alice has just realized something. What is it, and why is it important to the story? Try writing a thought bubble that shows what's going through her mind.

Why are there dotted lines in this panel? How do they connect to the text?

How has Alice changed since she first started at Wonderland? Do you think she'll reach her goal of being a super-skilled secret agent?

AUTHOR

Katie Schenkel is a comic writer best known for the critically acclaimed, Eisner Award-nominated graphic novel *The Cardboard Kingdom*. She especially loves to write about girls' friendships and their perspectives on the world around them. Midwest to her core, Katie lives in Chicago with her partner, Madison.

ILLUSTRATOR

Fern Cano is an illustrator born in Mexico City, Mexico. He currently resides in Monterrey, Mexico, where he makes a living as an illustrator and colorist. He has done work for Marvel, DC Comics, and role-playing games like Pathfinder from Paizo Publishing. In his spare time, he enjoys hanging out with friends, singing, rowing, and drawing!

GLOSSARY

agent (AY-juhnt)—a person who secretly works for a government or other group

code name (KOHD NAYM)—a name that is used in order to keep a person's real name secret

design (di-ZINE)—to plan out and make something for a specific use

expert (EK-spurt)—a person who has a lot of knowledge in something

free will (FREE WIL)—the ability to choose how you act

heiress (AIR-iss)—a woman who has gotten or will get the belongings of someone once they die; usually the belongings are very valuable things such as a large amount of money, ownership of a company, or land

intern (IN-turn)—a person who is working at a job in order to gain experience; usually an intern is a student or has just finished school

invisible (in-VIZ-uh-buhl)—impossible to see

mad (MAD)—thinking and acting in a strange, unusual way

martial arts (MAR-shuhl ARTS)—styles of fighting to protect yourself or to attack

mission (MISH-uhn)—an important job given to a person or group

shrink (SHRINGK)—to become or make smaller

traitor (TRAY-tuhr)—a person who is secretly helping the enemy

OLD FAVORITES. NEW SPINS.

FAR OUT CLASSIC STORIES